An Egg-cellent Costume Party!

By Bonnie Ventura
Illustrated by Leire Martín

A GOLDEN BOOK • NEW YORK

Licensed by:

HASBRO and its logo, MY LITTLE PONY, and all related characters are trademarks of Hasbro
and are used with permission.
© 2018 Hasbro. All Rights Reserved.

Published in the United States by Golden Books, an imprint of Random House Children's Books,
a division of Penguin Random House LLC, 1745 Broadway, New York, NY 10019, and in Canada by
Penguin Random House Canada Limited, Toronto. Golden Books, A Go'
the G colophon, and the distinctive gold spine are registered trademar

rhcbooks.com

ISBN 978-0-525-57858-1(trade) – ISBN 978-0-525-

Printed in the United States of America

10 9 8 7 6 5 4 3 2 1

D1416635

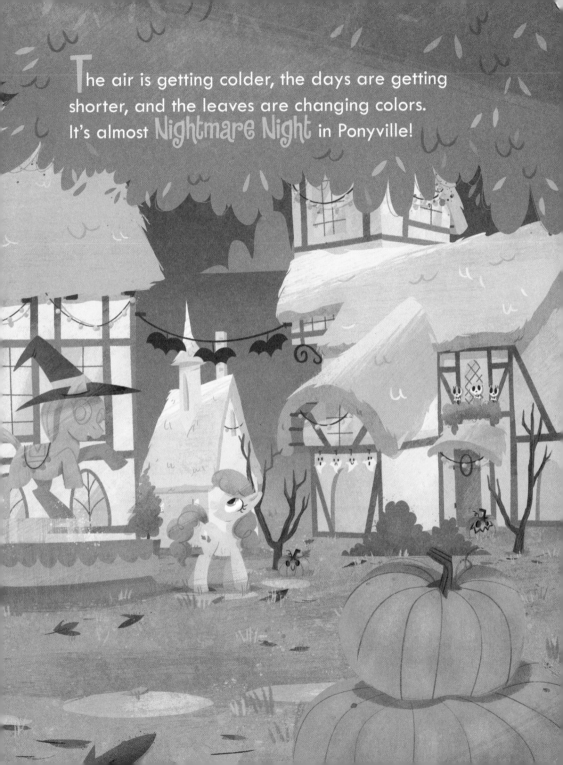

The air is getting colder, the days are getting shorter, and the leaves are changing colors. It's almost *Nightmare Night* in Ponyville!

This year, Pinkie Pie is throwing a party to celebrate the holiday. "It's going to be the **biggest** night before Nightmare Night party **ever**!" she exclaims.

She sends invitations to all her friends and
promises them . . .

. . . candy,

apple bobbing,

candy,

a scavenger hunt,

candy,

a costume contest,

and candy!

Everypony is **SO** excited! Pinkie always throws the **best parties.**

But her guests all have the same big problem.
Everypony wants to **win** the **costume contest** . . .
but they don't know what to wear!

Is the best night before Nightmare Night costume **sweet**?

Or is it scary?

Is it funny?

Or is it glamorous?

There is not a lot of time to decide!

Soon, the big celebration is here. Pinkie Pie rushes around, putting finishing touches on all the decorations. She has found the perfect costume. She is dressed like an **egg**!

Pinkie Pie's guests start to arrive!

As she welcomes everypony to her night before Nightmare Night party, she notices something amazing.

Everypony is a different kind of **chicken**!
Pinkie Pie has never seen so many chicken
costumes in her life! She is so excited!

But the rest of the ponies are stunned. Why are there so many chickens? The music stops and everypony looks at the egg.

"Rarity, you are such a fancy chicken! **I LOVE IT!**"

"A country chicken is such a **great** costume, Applejack!"

"*The Little Red Hen* is my favorite book of all time, Granny Smith! How did you know? Did I tell you?"

"Who doesn't love baby chicks?!" Pinkie cheers in almost one breath.

"Pip! **Egg-cellent** costume!"

Princess Twilight Sparkle laughs as Pinkie Pie continues to bounce with joy. "Everypony remembers the Nightmare Night you dressed up like a chicken! I guess we all thought the best way to win your contest was to be a chicken, too!"

"Yes, darling. You are simply an inspiration to us all!" says Rarity.

"Yeah, Pinkie. You're always the most fun,"
adds Fluttershy as she hugs her friend.

"It also explains the egg!" Rainbow Dash giggles.

"Aw, wow, thank you, everypony! This is going to be the biggest blast since the invention of the party cannon! It's the night before Nightmare Night!" exclaims Pinkie Pie.

DJ Pon-3 turns up the music and the party goes into full swing. Ponies munch on candy, bob for apples, and hunt for treasure.

Soon, it's time to announce the winner of the costume contest.

"Attention, everychicken!" Pinkie Pie shouts. "The winner of the Best Night Before Nightmare Night Costume Contest is . . . everychicken! There's no way I could choose just one chicken, so I choose you all!"

The crowd goes wild!

The fun lasts late into the night. After all, Pinkie knows that the secret to every great party is friends—and candy!